Karen's Newspaper

Look for these
and other books about Karen
in the
Baby-sitters Little Sister series:

1 Karen's Witch
2 Karen's Roller Skates
3 Karen's Worst Day
4 Karen's Kittycat Club
5 Karen's School Picture
6 Karen's Little Sister
7 Karen's Birthday
8 Karen's Haircut
9 Karen's Sleepover
#10 Karen's Grandmothers
#11 Karen's Prize
#12 Karen's Ghost
#13 Karen's Surprise
#14 Karen's New Year
#15 Karen's in Love
#16 Karen's Goldfish
#17 Karen's Brothers
#18 Karen's Home Run
#19 Karen's Good-bye
#20 Karen's Carnival
#21 Karen's New Teacher
#22 Karen's Little Witch
#23 Karen's Doll
#24 Karen's School Trip
#25 Karen's Pen Pal
#26 Karen's Ducklings

#27 Karen's Big Joke
#28 Karen's Tea Party
#29 Karen's Cartwheel
#30 Karen's Kittens
#31 Karen's Bully
#32 Karen's Pumpkin Patch
#33 Karen's Secret
#34 Karen's Snow Day
#35 Karen's Doll Hospital
#36 Karen's New Friend
#37 Karen's Tuba
#38 Karen's Big Lie
#39 Karen's Wedding
#40 Karen's Newspaper
#41 Karen's School

Super Specials:
1 Karen's Wish
2 Karen's Plane Trip
3 Karen's Mystery
4 Karen, Hannie, and
       Nancy: The Three
       Musketeers
5 Karen's Baby
6 Karen's Campout

Little Sister

Karen's Newspaper
Ann M. Martin

Illustrations by Susan Tang

A
LITTLE APPLE
PAPERBACK

SCHOLASTIC INC.
New York Toronto London Auckland Sydney

If you purchased this book without a cover, you should be aware that this book is stolen property. It was reported as "unsold and destroyed" to the publisher, and neither the author nor the publisher has received any payment for this "stripped book."

No part of this publication may be reproduced in whole or in part, or stored in a retrieval system, or transmitted in any form or by any means, electronic, mechanical, photocopying, recording, or otherwise, without written permission of the publisher. For information regarding permission, write to Scholastic Inc., 730 Broadway, New York, NY 10003.

ISBN 0-590-47040-X

Copyright © 1993 by Ann M. Martin. All rights reserved. Published by Scholastic Inc. APPLE PAPERBACKS ® and BABY-SITTERS LITTLE SISTER ® are registered trademarks of Scholastic Inc.

12 11 10 9 8 7 6 5 4 3 2 1   3 4 5 6 7 8/9

Printed in the U.S.A.   40

First Scholastic printing, August 1993

For Allison Poulos

The Stoneybrook News

"Mommy! Andrew is doing it again! He is saying it wrong. He is calling the grapes 'gapes.' That is not the right name."

"Karen, don't worry about it," said Mommy. "When Andrew is ready, he will say 'grapes.' After all, you used to call ice cream 'ackaminnie,' and you do not say that anymore."

"Thank goodness," I replied.

I am Karen Brewer. I am seven. I can read and write. Andrew is my brother. He is only four. He goes to preschool. Actually, when school starts in September, he will be going to a different preschool than the one he went to last year. That sounds very exciting. I just love new things. I love school, too. Especially my school. It is called Stoneybrook Academy. My two best friends go to Stoneybrook Academy with me. But right now we are having summer vacation. (I like vacation, too.)

Andrew and I were at our mother's house. It was a Thursday afternoon. Mommy had invited a friend over. She and her friend were going to have iced tea and fresh fruit on the back porch. Mommy said that was perfect for a hot summer day. She also said Andrew and I could join them, as long as we let them have a nice visit. She meant we should not squabble or whine or be pests. Andrew said he would rather paint pictures at the easel. But I wanted to meet Mommy's friend. She is a writer.

Mommy's friend is Mrs. Halsey. I waited until she was seated on the porch. I waited until Mommy had poured her a glass of iced tea. Then I said in a very grown-up voice, "So tell me, Mrs. Halsey. What kind of writing do you do?"

Mrs. Halsey smiled. "I write for our newspaper, Karen," she replied. "I write articles for the *Stoneybrook News*."

"You do?" I exclaimed. Boy. That was interesting. Everybody here in Stoneybrook, Connecticut, reads the *Stoneybrook News*. Well, the adults do. "Are you famous?" I asked Mrs. Halsey.

"I don't know about that," she said. "But my name is in the paper almost every week. You can find it in the masthead and also in my byline. I am a news reporter."

"What is a masthead?" I asked. "And what is a byline?"

"I will show you." Mrs. Halsey pulled a copy of the newspaper out of her bag. "Here is the masthead," she said. She pointed to a box near the front of the paper. Inside the box was a list of the people who work on the paper and the jobs they do. "And here is my byline," she went on.

"Right here where it says 'By Randi Halsey, staff writer and reporter.' I wrote this article."

Mrs. Halsey had turned to another page. She was pointing to an article called "Packaging Control Law Plan." I did not know what that was, so I tried to read the article. But the words were hard. Also, the story was boring. I turned the page. I tried to read some other articles. They were just as hard and boring as Mrs. Halsey's.

"Mrs. Halsey?" I said. "Excuse me. Excuse me, Mommy. Mrs. Halsey, the paper is kind of b — kind of, um, hard to read."

"Well, it is really for adults," said Mrs. Halsey.

Hmm. That did not seem fair at all.

Still, I like writing. And I have seen reporters on television. I think I would like to try being a reporter. But I guess I will have to wait until I am old enough to write boring, hard-to-read articles.

The Two-Two Summer

Andrew and I were having an interesting summer. We had done lots of things. I had been in a wedding. I had gone to overnight camp with my best friends. And Andrew and I had taken trips with our families. We have two families. We are part of a little family in Mommy's little house, and we are part of a big family in Daddy's big house. This is why.

When Andrew and I were much younger, we were part of just one family. Daddy, Mommy, Andrew, and me. We lived together in Daddy's house. (It is the house he grew up in.) But Mommy and Daddy fought a lot. After awhile they decided to get a divorce. They loved Andrew and me very much, but they did not love each other anymore. So Mommy moved into a little house. It is not very far from Daddy's house. And Andrew and I went with her.

Guess what happened after that. Mommy and Daddy got married again. But not to each other. Mommy married Seth. He is my stepfather. Daddy married Elizabeth. She is my stepmother. Now Andrew and I live with Daddy at the big house every other weekend, and on certain vacations and holidays. The rest of the time we live with Mommy at the little house.

This is my little-house family: Mommy, Seth, Andrew, me, Rocky, Midgie, and Emily Junior. Rocky and Midgie are Seth's cat and dog. They are okay, I guess, but their names are dumb. Emily Junior is my own pet rat.

This is my big-house family: Daddy, Elizabeth, Andrew, me, Nannie, Kristy, Sam, Charlie, David Michael, Emily Michelle, Boo-Boo, Shannon, Goldfishie, and Crystal Light the Second. Nannie is Elizabeth's mother, so she is my stepgrandmother. She helps take care of all us kids. Kristy, Sam, Charlie, and David Michael are Elizabeth's kids from her first marriage, before she knew Daddy. They are my stepsister and stepbrothers. Kristy is thirteen and a gigundoly excellent baby-sitter. I adore Kristy. Sam and Charlie are old. They go to high school. David Michael is seven like me, but he does not go to Stoneybrook Academy. Emily Michelle is my adopted sister. Daddy and Elizabeth adopted her from the country of Vietnam. She is two and a half. (I named my rat after her.) Boo-Boo is Daddy's cross old tomcat. Shannon is David Michael's puppy. She is quite large for someone who is supposed to be a puppy. And last of all are Goldfishie and Crystal Light the Second. (Guess what they are.) They belong to Andrew and me. Andrew named Goldfishie.

I made up special nicknames for my brother and me. I call us Andrew Two-Two and Karen Two-Two. (I got the idea for those names from the book *Jacob Two-Two Meets the Hooded Fang*.) We are two-twos because we have two of so many things. We have two houses and two families, two mommies and two daddies, two cats and two dogs. I have two bicycles, one at each house. I have two stuffed kitties that look just the same — Moosie at the big house, and Goosie at the little house. I even have two pieces of Tickly, my special blanket. Plus, Andrew and I have clothes and books and toys at each house. This is helpful because we go back and forth a lot, but we do not have to pack much each time.

Guess what else I have two of. Best friends. (The ones who go to school with me, remember?) They are Nancy Dawes and Hannie Papadakis. Nancy lives next door to Mommy. Hannie lives across the street from Daddy and one house down. I am lucky to have a best friend nearby, no matter which family I'm living with. In fact, I think I am mostly very lucky. I love both of my families a lot. And I know they love me.

The Boring Newspaper

Yawn, yawn, yawn.

It was Saturday morning and I could lie in bed for as long as I wanted. But I was at the big house, so I did not want to lie around for *too* long. I like to get up and see what's going on. The big house is an interesting place. Especially if you like people and animals.

I peered at the clock in my room. Seven-thirty. Not everyone would be awake yet. Certain people like to sleep late.

I tiptoed downstairs and into the kitchen.

I saw Daddy, Elizabeth, Nannie, and Andrew.

"Morning, everybody," I said cheerfully.

"Good morning," they replied.

And Andrew said, "This cereal box is really interesting." Andrew is very proud because he can read. I am proud, too. I taught him myself.

I sat down at the table. I popped a slice of bread in the toaster.

Rattle, rattle. All the grown-ups were reading newspapers. They were reading three different papers. The sections they were not reading were lying on the counter. I took a couple of sections for myself. I read the headlines while I waited for my toast. "School Budget Cuts Increase," said one. (I thought that article might be interesting because "school" was in the title, but I was wrong.) "Community Leaders Rally for Trip to Capital" looked interesting, too, but it turned out not to be a story about a field trip.

I could not find anything interesting in the papers.

While I ate my toast, I looked around the table. Andrew was still reading the cereal box. The grown-ups were still reading the papers. Finally I stood up. I found my copy of *Henry and Ribsy* by Beverly Cleary. I sat down with it. Now I could read, too.

"Elizabeth," said Daddy a few minutes later, "these budget cuts are appalling. Did you read this article?"

"Yes," said Elizabeth, "and you are right. We need a new school board."

"Who here has read *Henry and Ribsy*?" I asked. (No one heard me.)

"Look at this," said Nannie. "The mayor of the town of Lawrenceville has okayed a site for a dump."

"I bet the residents are unhappy," said Daddy.

"Ribsy is a dog, in case anyone does not know," I said.

"You know what's wrong with this world?" asked Nannie.

"Yes," I replied. "The newspapers are gigundoly boring."

This time everyone heard me. They laughed.

"Sorry, Karen," said Daddy. "We did not mean to ignore you and Andrew."

"That's all right," I replied. "But these papers really are boring."

"I think they are written for adults," said Elizabeth.

"That is what Mrs. Halsey told me," I said.

"Kids can read other things," remarked Andrew. "Like cereal boxes."

"Or books. There are plenty of books for kids," I said.

Nannie stood up. She carried her plate to the sink. "What is everybody going to do today?" she asked.

"I am going to work in the garden," said Daddy.

"I need to run errands," said Elizabeth.

14

"Can I invite a friend over?" Andrew wanted to know.

"I think so," said Daddy. "Who do you have in mind?"

"Ryan. He went to my old school."

"Great," said Daddy. "You can call him as soon as you finish eating."

That was nice, I thought. Soon Andrew would make new friends at his new school. And he could still see his old friends. I decided to invite my two best friends over.

Karen's Newspaper

My two best friends could not come over. At least not right away. Hannie had gone to the dentist, and nobody answered when I telephoned Nancy.

The big house was a busy place. Sam and Charlie ran around making plans. Then they left in the Junk Bucket. (That is the name of Charlie's car.) Kristy invited her friends Mary Anne and Stacey over. They closed themselves into the den and would not come out. I think they were calling boys on the phone. David Michael ran across the street to look for Linny Papadakis. (Linny is Hannie's older brother.) Then he and Linny came back. They tossed a football around in the yard. And Ryan showed up to play with Andrew. They ran through the sprinkler in their swimming trunks.

I waited for Hannie. I called Nancy again. No answer. So I dragged all those newspapers onto the front steps. I sat down with them. I decided *some*thing interesting must be in them *some*where.

I turned the pages slowly. I saw headlines with words in them like "government" and "politics" and "dynamics" and "courtroom." I saw ads for furniture and grown-up clothes. I saw lists of cars and houses for sale. Boring, boring, boring.

And then I saw it. A crossword puzzle! At last — something for kids. I leaped to my feet. I ran inside and all the way upstairs to my room. I looked through my desk for a pencil. (Doing a crossword puzzle with a pen is not a good idea. If you make a mistake, it is very hard to erase ink.)

I found a pencil with a good eraser. Then I raced back to the crossword puzzle. The squares in it were very tiny. I would have to use my smallest, neatest printing. But that was okay.

The first Across clue was "Father of Cubism." Huh? I skipped to the next Across clue. It said, "A rite of passage." (Somebody had spelled "right" wrong.) Well, boo and bullfrogs. This puzzle was no fun. (Plus, the newspaper people could not spell.) In school we work on puzzles with clues like "Tiny picnic pests" or "What birds live in."

The newspaper even had boring crossword puzzles. I could not believe it.

"What are you doing?"

I looked up. Hannie was running across the yard.

"Hi!" I called. "I am trying to enjoy this paper, but I cannot. It is just for grown-ups. Even the puzzle. Look. I could not fill in one space."

Hannie stood there with her hands on her hips. She opened her mouth.

I opened my mouth.

And at the exact same time we said, "Let's start our own newspaper!"

We giggled.

Then I said, "We could, you know. We could do that."

"Don't we need grown-ups?" asked Hannie.

"Grown-ups are the *last* thing we need," I told her. "This will be a kids' newspaper. By kids and for kids." I paused. "I know just what to do."

"What?" asked Hannie.

"First we need to get the third Musketeer. Let's call Nancy."

We telephoned her again, and this time Nancy was at home.

"We are starting a kids' newspaper," I told her. "Hannie and I just had the idea. Do you want to help us?"

"Sure!" cried Nancy. "What do I do?"

"Can your mom or dad drive you to the big house?" I asked.

"I think so."

"Great. We will start as soon as you get here."

The 3M Gazette

Nancy and Hannie and I had lots to talk about. We sat under a tree in the backyard. (We sat far away from the sprinkler.)

"What will we write about in our newspaper?" asked Hannie.

"News. What else?" I replied.

"I know. But *what* news? Where will we get the news?"

"My parents get their news out of the grown-up newspaper," said Nancy.

"Well, we are *not* going to get our news from there," I said. "We will get it from wherever the newspaper people get it."

"I think they get it from reporters," said Hannie.

"We can be reporters!" cried Nancy.

"Yes!" I said. "We will report the news ourselves."

"The news from where?" asked Hannie.

"The news from right here. Our kids' paper will be for the big-house neighborhood. Everything that is happening here."

"We can talk to people in the neighborhood," added Nancy. "We can go to their doors and say we are writing a kids' paper, and ask if they have any interesting news for us."

"Plus, if something exciting happens, we can be on the scene," I added. "We will take notes and ask questions."

"Probing questions," said Nancy.

"Is our kids' paper going to be only *about* kids?" asked Hannie.

I thought for a moment. "No," I said at last. "It will be written by kids, and it will be interesting for kids to read. But it can be about kids or grown-ups or animals or anything."

"That's good," said Hannie. "Because I know some news about my father that we can put in the paper. We will not even have to go door-to-door for this story. I can just tell it to you, and then we can write about it."

"That's a great idea!" I exclaimed. "I know something about Charlie."

"And I know something about Mr. Billing," said Nancy. "Do you know the Billings? They live right down the street, so they are in this neighborhood."

"You know what we need to do next?" said Hannie. "We need to think of a name for our newspaper. What will we call it?"

"*The Neighborhood News*?" suggested Nancy.

"*The Stoneybrook Times*?" I suggested.

Hannie frowned. "Those names are okay, but they are not special. They sound like names for any old paper."

"Maybe we need a name that says something about kids," I said.

"Or about *us*," said Hannie.

"How about *The 3M Gazette*?" suggested Nancy.

"Three Em?" repeated Hannie.

"For the Three Musketeers."

"Perfect!" I cried. "Now for our jobs. We need someone to be a reporter, someone to be a writer, and someone to print the paper."

"I want to do everything," said Nancy.

"Me too," said Hannie.

We decided we would all be reporters and writers and printers.

"Where *are* we going to print the paper?" wondered Hannie.

"At the big house," I replied. "We can use the word processor. I use it a lot. Sam or Charlie or Kristy can help us if we get stuck. We can print out the copies on the printer. Then we will deliver one to each house in the neighborhood. I think our paper should be free."

Guess what. David Michael and Linny ran to us then and asked what we were doing. We told them about our paper. Then they asked if they could help us. So we said they could be our paperboys.

Reporters

We did not waste a second. Nancy and Hannie and I went right to work. We decided that we would be reporters that very afternoon.

"I think we should *look* like reporters, too," said Hannie. "People will take us more seriously if we do. They will give us better news."

"In that case, we will need hats," I said.

"And cigars," added Nancy.

"Cigars!" I cried. "We cannot carry cigars around. They are very, very bad for you."

"We would not *light* them," replied Nancy.

"Well, we do not know anyone who smokes cigars," I told her. "So we cannot borrow any. Thank goodness. Believe me, we do not need them. But we will wear hats. We can borrow them from Watson and your dad, Hannie. And we will stick pieces of paper under the bands. The papers will say PRESS on them. All the best reporters do that."

As soon as we had eaten lunch we were ready to go. Elizabeth said we could only ring the doorbells of people we know very well. We could not go to strangers' houses, even in the neighborhood. If we wanted to do that, a grown-up would have to come with us. We promised we would not visit any strangers.

Hannie and Nancy and I put on our PRESS hats. We found three pencils and three small pads of paper so we could take notes. We were ready to go.

"Whose house first?" asked Nancy.

"Melody's," replied Hannie.

So we walked across the str friend Melody Korman's house.

I rang the bell. Bill Korman ans He is Melody's big brother.

"Hi," I said. "We are — "

"What's with the hats?" interrupted Bill.

"We are reporters," I told him. "For a brand new kids' paper. *Our* paper. It is called *The 3M Gazette.* Do you have any news for us? We could write an article about you or your family."

"Well," said Bill slowly. He thought for a moment. "Yesterday we got a new blender. I guess that is all."

"Are you sure that is all?" asked Hannie. Bill nodded.

"Could we see the blender?" I wanted to know. (We would have to be able to describe it, and maybe say something special about it.)

Bill showed us the blender, and we took some notes. Then we left.

We rang the bell at the Kilbournes' next

door, but no one answered. So we rang Hannie's bell.

"Ah, the reporters," said her father. "Am I famous yet?"

"Not yet," said Hannie. (She giggled.) "Do you have any news?"

"Let me think. Sari just flushed a stuffed animal down the toilet." (Sari is Hannie's little sister.) "The plumbers are on their way over."

That was good. We went to the scene of the crime. We described what the bathroom looked like. We even waited for the plumbers, so we could write about the repair job and how much it cost.

Then we went to Timmy Hsu's house. Timmy is Chinese-American, and guess what. His grandparents were visiting all the way from the country of China. They were wearing very interesting clothes, and they were speaking Chinese. Even Timmy was speaking Chinese. (We did not know he could do that.) We took lots of notes at the Hsus' house.

When we left the Hsus', we went back to the Kilbournes' and then to my house. We thought about visiting Mrs. Porter who lives next door to me, but we know she is actually a witch, so we decided not to. Anyway, we already had enough news for the first issue of *The 3M Gazette*.

Andrew's School

Everybody at the big house was home for Saturday night dinner. But after dinner, people started to leave. Sam and Charlie had dates. Kristy went to Stacey's house for a sleepover. And Nannie went bowling. (She is very good. She plays on a team.)

I went upstairs. I wanted to read some more of *Henry and Ribsy*. As I was walking along the hall, I heard a sound.

Sniff, sniff. Sniffle, sniff.

"Andrew?" I said. I backed up. I peeked into his room.

Andrew was on his bed. He was crying, just sitting there crying.

I sat down next to him. "What is the matter?" I asked.

Andrew gulped. Tears were running down his cheeks. "Nothing," he said.

"But you are crying. Why are you crying?"

"Because . . ." Andrew paused. "Because I do not want to go to my new school."

"Why not?" I asked.

"Well, Ryan will not be there. I will not know *any* of the kids there. They will be new. Everything will be new. My teacher, the toys. Plus, I will not know where the bathroom is."

"But somebody will show you," I said. "You do not have to worry about that. Your new teacher will show you the bathroom and everything else on the first day."

"Maybe my new teacher will be mean."

"Maybe she won't."

"But she might be," wailed Andrew. "I want my old teacher. I miss her."

"Your new teacher might be your best teacher ever. And you will get to make new friends. I just love new friends. And who knows what could be on your new playground. Or what great toys you could find in your new classroom. Andrew, a new school is so exciting!"

"Not to me."

"Mommy and Daddy would not send you to this new school if they thought you would not like it."

Andrew shrugged his shoulders. He did not say anything. But at least he had stopped crying.

"I know what will make you feel better," I said to my brother. "I will be right back." I ran to my room. I found *Henry and Ribsy*. I brought it back to Andrew and began to read to him. I started over at the beginning so he would not miss a word.

Writers

On Saturday, Nancy and Hannie and I had been reporters. On Sunday, we became writers. We had a newspaper to put out.

My friends came over to my house again. We gathered around the computer. We looked at the news stories we had collected, our little pages of notes. We had twelve little pages all together.

"That is a lot of stories," said Nancy.

"Enough for a newspaper?" asked Hannie.

"I think so."

There were the stories we had collected door to door. Then there were those three stories we already knew about, the ones we had overheard.

"Let's write up our own stories first," I said. "The ones we do not have any notes on. Hannie, what is your story?"

"My father has gone on a diet," Hannie announced. "It was his idea. He says he needs to trim down. He wants to lose fifteen pounds. Then he will not have a spare tire around his middle."

"A spare tire?" I repeated.

"That is what he calls his fat."

"Oh. Okay."

My friends and I wrote two paragraphs about Hannie's father and his fat. We called the article "Spare Tire." We typed it on the keyboard. (Sam had helped us turn on the computer. He had shown us how to save our stories on a disk.)

"Great," I said when we finished "Spare Tire." "Now for my article. It is about Charlie. He bought a bracelet from a jewelry store last week. The bracelet is going to be a present for a girl. Charlie wants her to be his girlfriend. He hopes the bracelet will impress her. I heard him say so to Sam."

"Can we see the bracelet?" asked Hannie. "We should tell what it looks like. Maybe the tag will still be attached. Then we can tell the price, too."

The Three Musketeers sneaked into Charlie's room. We found the bracelet *and* the price tag. The bracelet did not seem expensive to me, but what do I know about good jewelry? We called the article "Charlie's Five-Dollar Bracelet."

"Now for my story," said Nancy. "My story about Mr. Billing. Okay. I know for a fact he was fired from his job. I just happened to be listening on the phone when Mrs. Billing was talking to Mommy."

"Hey! That is big news! Thanks, Nancy," I said. The title of this article was "Mr. Billing Loses Job!!"

After that we wrote about the Kormans'

blender and Timmy's grandparents. Then we wrote that Boo-Boo had been to the vet for his shots. Then we wrote a short article to remind people that Kristy and her friends run a baby-sitting business.

"See?" I said when we had finished writing the articles. "This is a paper kids will *want* to read. Look at our headlines. No long words. No boring words either, like 'dynamics' or 'sewage treatment.' And plenty of exclamation points. They always make things look more interesting. I think our best one is 'Mr. Billing Loses Job!!' "

Nancy and Hannie agreed with me.

"Okay," said Nancy. "Now let's print out one copy of our paper to see how it looks. I wonder how long it is."

It turned out to be four pages long. And it looked very nice, except that it had no pictures. We would have to work on that.

We printed out fifteen more copies of our paper. We stapled the pages together. The first issue of *The 3M Gazette* was finished.

Paperboys

"We need our paperboys," I said. Hannie and Nancy and I were standing on the front steps of the big house. We were holding *The 3M Gazette*. It was ready to be delivered.

"Oh, paperboys!" I shouted.

"Oh, paperboys!" shouted Hannie and Nancy.

A few minutes later, David Michael and Linny ran around the side of the house. They had been playing football again. They were sweaty.

"You called?" said Linny.

"*The 3M Gazette* is ready to be delivered," I announced.

David Michael dropped the football. "It is?" he said. "Cool!"

"Can we look at it before we deliver it?" asked Linny.

"Of course," I replied. "Delivery boys get a sneak peek."

David Michael and Linny each took a copy of the paper. They sat on the grass and read it. They smiled a lot.

"Can Timmy really speak Chinese?" asked Linny.

"Did Charlie really buy a bracelet to impress a girl?" wondered David Michael. He snickered. "What a waste."

"Hannie, you told about Dad's spare tire?" said Linny. He looked at his sister. "Hmm. I am not sure — hey, cool! You wrote about Sari, too. Our family is famous."

"So are you guys ready to deliver the papers?" I asked. I was feeling impatient.

I wanted to see what other kids thought about *The 3M Gazette*. It was time for the paperboys to get to work.

David Michael stood up. "We're ready," he said. "What is the pay?"

"Excuse me?"

"How much are you going to pay us?" asked David Michael.

I looked at Nancy and Hannie. Then I looked at the boys. "We were not going to pay you anything," I replied.

"Well, why did you think we wanted to work for you?" asked Linny.

"Because you like our paper?" suggested Nancy.

"Because you like us?" suggested Hannie. "And because you are so wonderful and helpful and good and kind?"

Linny made a face at his sister.

"Why *did* you offer to work for us?" I asked.

"Because we are broke," replied David Michael. "We need bucks."

"But *The 3M Gazette* is a free paper. We

43

are not charging money for it," I explained. "We are just having fun."

"And we are doing something good for the children of this neighborhood," added Hannie. "Don't you want to be part of that?"

David Michael and Linny looked at each other. They shrugged.

Linny said, "What a gyp."

And David Michael said, "No fair."

"All right. We will deliver the papers ourselves," I told them.

David Michael held up his hand. "Nah," he said. "Don't bother. Linny and I will deliver them. We do not have anything better to do."

So the boys took the stack of papers. They ran to the sidewalk. Then they walked up and down the street calling, "Free paper for sale!" They handed out papers to all the kids they saw.

My friends and I went back to the computer.

"This was a lot of work," said Hannie.

"But it was fun," added Nancy.

"You know what?" I said. "If we collect news and write some more articles this week, we can put out another issue of the paper next Saturday or Sunday. *The 3M Gazette* can be a weekly paper."

Privacy

That evening, Andrew and I returned to the little house. I was very tired. Hannie was right. Publishing a paper was a lot of work. When supper was over, the only thing I wanted to do was read. But I did not have a chance. That was because of the phone calls.

Charlie was the first to call.

"Karen?" he said when I had picked up the phone. "I just want to say thanks. Thanks a whole lot." Charlie did not sound thankful at all. He sounded angry.

"Um, what for?" I asked.

"I just read *The 3M Gazette*. Who said you could write an article about that bracelet and my girlfriend? And how did you find out how much the bracelet cost? I did not tell you any of those things."

"Well," I began.

"You had no right," Charlie went on. "That is my private business. I do not want people to know I am trying to impress Ellen. Sam has been laughing at me all evening. I hope Ellen does not see your paper."

Oops. I had not thought about that.

"Charlie, I'm sorry," I said. "Really, really, really, gigundoly sorry."

As soon as Charlie and I were finished talking, the phone rang again. This time Hannie was calling. "Karen," she said, "Daddy did not like my article. The one about his spare tire."

"He didn't?"

"No. He is very embarrassed. He said his diet and his fat are his own personal business. He said family things are not supposed to be published in papers for all the world to see."

"But he let us write about Sari and the toilet," I said.

"I know. He told us we could do that. But he did not know we were going to write about his fat. I think we should have asked first."

The third person to call that night was Nancy. She sounded as if she might be crying. She kept sniffling.

"Is something wrong?" I asked her.

"Mommy and Daddy are mad," she said. "They read our paper."

"Uh-oh. And they did not like the story about Mr. Papadakis, right?"

"Wrong. They did not like the story about Mr. Billing," replied Nancy.

"Wasn't it true?" I asked. "Didn't he get fired?"

"Yes, but that was supposed to be a secret for a few more days. They had not told most of their friends yet. Just Mommy and

Daddy. Plus, I was not supposed to be eavesdropping on the phone. Now I have to call the Billings and say I'm sorry. And my mom wants to talk to your mom."

I had a feeling I might be in trouble.

Mommy talked to Mrs. Dawes for a long time. After a while, Seth got on another phone, and he talked to them, too. When everyone finally hung up, Mommy said, "Karen, may we see *The 3M Gazette*, please?"

I had brought one copy to the little house with me. I handed it to Mommy. She and Seth read it together. Then Mommy said, "Karen, I think we need to talk. How did you get these stories?"

"Well, Hannie and Nancy and I walked around the neighborhood. We interviewed people. For most of the stories," I added. "Some of the stories we just wrote down by ourselves."

"Like the story about Mr. Billing?" asked Mommy. I nodded. "Honey," she went on, "your paper is wonderful, but you must respect people's privacy. Do you understand what that means?"

"I do now," I replied. "Mommy, I did not mean to hurt anybody's feelings. Honest. I know we have to change our paper. The next issue will be different. That is a promise." I crossed my heart.

After-shave

Nancy and Hannie and I decided not to work on our paper on Monday. We had planned to get some more news stories that day, but we changed our minds. We thought that might not be a very good idea, since several people were mad at us. *The 3M Gazette* needed a rest.

My friends and I did something different on Monday. We wrote three letters. One was to Charlie, one was to Hannie's father, and one was to Mr. and Mrs. Billing. They were "I'm sorry" letters. We wrote the letters together. (Mommy helped us with the spelling.) We used Nancy's best flowered notepaper.

This is what Charlie's letter said:

DEAR CHARLIE,

WE ARE VERY, VERY SORRY WE WROTE ABOUT YOU IN OUR NEWSPAPER. WE WROTE ABOUT YOU EVEN THOUGH WE DID NOT HAVE YOUR PERMISSION. WE WILL NOT DO THAT AGAIN BECAUSE WE DO NOT WANT TO HURT YOUR FEELINGS. AND WE WANT YOU TO KEEP ON READING THE 3M GAZETTE.

WE REALLY ARE SORRY.

LOVE,
KAREN, NANCY, AND HANNIE
THE THREE MUSKETEERS

The letters to Mr. Papadakis and the Billings were pretty much like the letter to Charlie. Except on the Billings' letter we wrote "very" six times before we wrote "sorry." Then we mailed the letters.

"You know something?" said Hannie when we were walking to the mailbox. "I asked my mom and dad what freedom of speech means. They said it means in this country people are free to say or write whatever they think. There is no law against it."

"But if you do not want to hurt people, you have to be careful about what you say," I replied.

"Right," agreed Nancy. "It was not really important for everyone to know about Hannie's father's spare tire, so we did not need to write that article. It is more important to respect his privacy."

"We will know better next time," I said.

On Tuesday we decided it was safe to interview people for the next issue of *The 3M Gazette*. So my friends and I put on our PRESS hats. We found our pencils and our pads of paper.

"Remember," I said, "we will only write about what people *tell* us we can write about."

We went to Timmy Hsu's house first.

"We are going to get a puppy," said Timmy. "A golden retriever."

Then we went to the Kilbournes' house.

"I won a swimming trophy," said Maria proudly. "I will show it to you."

After that we went to Mr. Giordano's house, but he was not home, so we went back to the big house. David Michael was in the yard with Emily Michelle.

"Do you have any news for *The 3M Gazette*?" I asked him.

David Michael grinned. "I ordered some after-shave through the mail," he replied. "I saw an ad for it in the back of a magazine."

"Why do you want after-shave?" I wanted to know. "You do not shave yet."

"I want to smell good."

Hmm. We had not found very interesting news this time.

"Nobody *told* us anything too interesting," said Hannie.

"Maybe we could make it *sound* interesting," I said. "We could write headlines in capital letters with lots of exclamation points. Like this: 'DAVID MICHAEL ORDERS AFTER-SHAVE!!!!' "

"At least we will not get in trouble," said Nancy.

"Right," I agreed. "Okay, it is time for all reporters to take a break. Tomorrow we will be writers again. Get ready to use the computer."

Across and Down

Saturday was the beginning of a little-house weekend. But guess where I went first thing that morning. To the big house.

Mommy dropped Nancy and me off at Daddy's on her way downtown to run errands. "Mrs. Dawes will pick you up at four o'clock this afternoon," she reminded us. Then she drove away.

"Let's get Hannie," I said. "We have a lot to do today."

The Three Musketeers were very busy at

the computer. First we wrote up the news stories we had collected.

"Let's print out one copy and see how the paper looks," suggested Nancy.

So we did. This time our paper was only two pages long.

I studied it. "It *needs* something," I said.

"Pictures?" said Hannie.

"Pictures might help," I agreed.

We called for Sam. He showed us how the computer could illustrate our stories. We added a drawing of a trophy next to the article about Maria Kilbourne, and a drawing of a puppy next to the article about Timmy Hsu. (We did not know what to do about David Michael's article.)

After that we printed out another copy of the paper.

"Better," I said. Then I remembered something. "The crossword puzzle!" I cried. "The awful crossword puzzle."

"What?" said Hannie and Nancy.

"Our paper needs a puzzle. Other papers have them," I said. "But we need a fun puzzle for kids. Come on. Let's make one."

"*Make* one?" repeated Hannie. "We can't do that."

"I bet we can," said Nancy. "Let's try."

We found some graph paper. We began writing words in the squares. Across and down. All of our words were about summertime.

"Let's put in 'vacation,' " said Hannie. "And 'swimming.' "

"How about 'picnic'?" suggested Nancy.

Fitting those across words with those down words was hard. Then we had to write clues for them. Then Sam had to show us how to put the puzzle on the computer so we could print it out.

"Couldn't you guys do something easy?" he said. "Like design a spaceship?"

"This is important," I replied. Then I remembered to add, "Thank you very much."

A little while later, the paperboys were delivering the second issue of *The 3M Gazette*.

The Supermarket Papers

On Sunday, Nancy and I went over to Hanna's house. Mr. Dawes drove us. We wanted to find out what the kids in the big-house neighborhood thought about the new issue of *The 3M Gazette*. (Also, we wanted to know if we were in trouble for anything.)

The Three Musketeers decided to poll the kids who were reading our paper. First we talked to Linny Papadakis.

"What did you think of your new copy of *The 3M Gazette*?" I asked him. (I was ready with paper and a pencil, in case I needed to write down anything he said.) "What is your honest opinion?" I added.

"Well," said Linny slowly, "it was . . . it was . . . I liked the puzzle."

"Hmm. And what about the articles?" I asked.

"They were okay."

Next we went across the street to Daddy's house. We asked David Michael the same questions.

"My *honest* opinion?" he said. "Well, it was, um, a little boring. But I liked the puzzle. That was fun."

Guess what. Timmy Hsu said the same thing. So did Melody Korman. Well, bullfrogs. We could not please anyone. First the paper caused trouble. Now it was boring.

"But you could make it interesting," said Melody. "That would be easy."

"You mean use more exclamation points?" asked Hannie.

Melody shook her head. "No. Make it

like the papers at the checkout counter in the supermarket. They are *really* interesting."

I turned to Hannie and Nancy. "If that is true then we have to get to the grocery store. Right now! It is an emergency. Come on. I think Nannie is going there today."

We ran back to the big house. Sure enough, Nannie was holding a shopping list. She was just about to climb into her car, the Pink Clinker.

"Please can we ride with you?" I asked.

"If you tell your parents where you are going," Nannie replied.

Twenty minutes later, the Three Musketeers were crowded around a rack of newspapers in the supermarket. (Nannie was walking up and down the aisles with a shopping cart.)

Nancy opened a paper called *The National Star*. "Here is an article about a little boy who has x-ray vision. His eyes are red, and he can see through walls." She turned a page. "And here is a story about a man

who is a real vampire. Ew, look!" she shrieked. "There's his picture! Look at his fangs!"

Hannie opened another paper. It was called *The Weekly Tattletale*. She read us some headlines. They were "Formerly Bald Man Grows Moss on Forehead" and "Ancient Statue Cries Real Tears" and "Woman Gives Birth to Alien — Baby Has Green Skin."

Then I looked at a paper called *Eye on the World*. The very first story in it was about a man who said his cat had been kidnapped by Martians.

"I wonder if he knows the woman with the alien baby," said Hannie.

My friends giggled.

"Is there a picture of the Martians taking the kitty?" asked Nancy.

"No," I replied. "But here is a picture of a grandmother who arm wrestled with a bank robber."

"Ready to go, girls?" asked Nannie. She

was standing behind us. Her shopping cart was full.

"I guess so," I replied. "Hannie? Nancy? How much money do you have? I think we should buy some of these papers."

We emptied our pockets. We had just enough money to buy *The National Star* and *Eye on the World*. I knew they would be helpful.

Psychic Mom Saves
Son from Bigfoot

Hannie and Nancy and I returned to Hannie's house. We went to her bedroom. We opened our newspapers. We studied the stories.

We read about two people who said the fillings in their teeth could pick up radio stations. They heard music in their mouths. We read about *lots* of aliens. We read about people who set weird records. We read about a baby who weighed twenty-eight pounds when she was born.

Finally Hannie said, "I wonder if these

stories are true. I remember when my mom had Sari. Sari weighed six pounds. I do not think a brand-new baby could weigh twenty-eight pounds."

"And I do not think Martians would travel all the way to Earth just to kidnap a cat," said Nancy. "Don't you think they would want something bigger?"

"The articles must be made up," I said. "They have to be."

"But newspaper stories are supposed to be true," said Hannie.

"Maybe not," said Nancy. "Maybe we were wrong about that."

"Well, we can make up stories as well as anyone else can," I said. "Boy. Melody was right. We can make *The 3M Gazette* much more interesting."

During the next week, the Three Musketeers worked hard. We wrote lots of interesting articles for our paper. They were all made up.

Nancy thought up the best headline. It was PSYCHIC MOM SAVES SON FROM BIG-

FOOT!!! (We had noticed a lot of articles about Bigfoot in those papers.) To go with it, we made up a story about a mother who could see the future. She used a Ouija board to receive messages from the Beyond. One of the messages was about her little boy, Billy, and how Bigfoot was going to attack him on Halloween, so she decided not to let him go trick-or-treating. That way, Bigfoot could not get to him. She had saved her dear son's life.

Another good headline was FIFTY-NINE-POUND GOLDFISH STUCK IN OWN TANK! Hannie made up a story about how a pet goldfish had kept on growing and growing, but his owner did not notice. Finally the fish weighed fifty-nine pounds. It was so big it filled up its whole tank. The owner had to break the tank to get the fish out.

Then I wrote a story about a man with magical powers who could make clocks run backward. I called it MAGIC MAN SAVES TIME!!

On Wednesday, the Three Musketeers

were sitting in Hannie's backyard. We were making up a story about a little girl who never cut her fingernails and now they were three feet long.

"Hey! You guys!" called Linny. He was running across the lawn. "I have a story for your paper. Want to hear it?"

"Well . . ." I said. My friends and I had not thought about collecting boring *real* stories. We were just going to invent interesting fake ones.

"What is the story?" asked Nancy.

"I just found out that my best friend and I are going to be in the same class in school this year. We were hoping that would happen. I know everyone is going to want to read *that* story."

A little while later, Maria Kilbourne came over. "I won another trophy," she announced. "Next week I will be in the final swim meet."

Then Timmy Hsu walked his new puppy over. The puppy's name was Ghost. Timmy was very proud of her.

Hannie and Nancy and I made some notes about Linny and his best friend, and Maria and her trophy, and Timmy and Ghost. We wrote short articles about them. But the biggest headline on the third issue of *The 3M Gazette* was the one about the psychic mom. The rest of the articles were the made-up ones.

On Saturday, when the papers were finished, we gave them to our delivery boys. We could not wait to find out what everyone thought of our very interesting newspaper.

The Funny Papers

The weekend our interesting paper was delivered, Andrew and I were staying at the big house. After supper we sat in the living room. All of us. My entire big-house family.

"Did everybody see the new issue of *The 3M Gazette*?" I asked.

"Not me," said Sam.

"Not yet," said Nannie.

I had two extra copies of the paper. I passed them around. I smiled. I knew no one would be bored. Right away, they would see that great big headline: Psychic Mom Saves Son from Bigfoot!!! They would start reading, and they would not be able to stop.

Nannie took one copy of the paper. She read it while Kristy and Andrew and Daddy looked over her shoulders. Charlie and Elizabeth looked over Sam's shoulders. At first the living room was silent.

Then I heard a snicker. It had come from Charlie. "Psychic mom?" he murmured. He was smiling.

So were Kristy and Elizabeth and Daddy.

Charlie's face was turning red. He covered his mouth with his hand. Finally he laughed out loud.

"Charlie," said Elizabeth.

"Sorry. I can't help it," replied Charlie. He was laughing so hard tears were running down his cheeks.

Andrew nudged me. "Karen, why is Charlie crying?"

"Never mind," I replied.

Charlie could not stop laughing. He put

the paper down. Then he said, "Bigfoot. A fifty-nine-pound goldfish. Clocks running backward. This is better than the funny papers."

I looked around the room. Charlie was the only one laughing, but almost everyone else was hiding smiles. Only Andrew, Emily, and David Michael were not.

I stood up. "Well, I'm glad you think the paper is so funny," I said. I knew darn well that "funny papers" meant "comics." I was insulted. The Three Musketeers had worked very hard for a week. We had not done all that work just so everyone would laugh at our paper.

Kristy tried to stop smiling. "But Karen," she said, "what kind of a paper is this? You just made up these stories."

"Well, isn't that what the people who wrote *The National Star* and *Eye on the World* did? We made *The 3M Gazette* just like those papers."

"I don't know," replied Daddy. "Maybe they did make up the stories, maybe they didn't. But the point is that *you* did, Karen. You made up every word of most of these articles. That is not reporting, honey."

"Hannie *said* newspaper articles are supposed to be true," I told my family. "I guess she was right after all."

Andrew was still peering at the paper. "Karen, some of the stories are true. The story about Linny is. So are the ones about Timmy and Maria."

Sometimes I forget that Andrew can read. Most four-year-olds cannot read. But Andrew can. I thought of something. "Hey, Andrew," I said. "I bet you will be the only kid in your class at your new school who can read. Your teacher will like that."

Andrew stuck out his lower lip. "I am not going to that new school," he said.

I shrugged. I looked at *The 3M Gazette* again. My friends and I had worked hard and our paper *still* was not right. Well, I was not going to give up. We would just have to work even harder. I decided to go to bed early since I had so much to do.

Getting It Right

"My father laughed when he read about Bigfoot," said Hannie. "My mother kept poking him, and saying, 'George, George.' But he would not stop laughing." Hannie looked very huffy.

"My mother and father did not laugh," reported Nancy. "But I think they wanted to. And my mother said, 'Maybe fiction is stranger than truth after all.' I am not sure what she meant by that."

It was Sunday afternoon. Hannie and Nancy and I were in Hannie's backyard. I had just told my friends what had happened at the big house the night before. They were not in good moods.

But I was. "I thought about *The 3M Gazette* all night, and I have lots of new ideas," I announced. "I know just how to fix our paper."

"How?" asked Nancy. "We have tried telling the truth and we have tried making up stories. What's left?"

"Plenty," I replied. "I can think of lots of ways to make the paper more interesting. We just have to . . . to spice it up. The puzzle was a good way to start. Everyone likes the puzzle. I mean, all the kids do. The pictures were good, too. So what we have to do is keep telling the truth — "

"And only write about what we have permission to write about," added Hannie. "So we will not get in trouble again."

"Right," I agreed. "And add some fun things."

"More puzzles and pictures?" said Hannie.

"Yes, and other things, too. We could start a column called 'Letters from Readers.' Kids can write to us when they have something to say about the paper, and we will print their letters."

"Cool," said Nancy. "Hey, I have an idea. Every week we could let someone be a guest reporter. You know, like Timmy or Maria could write an article for the paper."

"We could have contests," suggested Hannie. "Draw the best picture or write the best story or tell the funniest joke."

"That's a good idea," said Nancy. "That way, kids will keep reading the paper to find out if they have won a contest."

"Maybe we could announce something big," I said slowly. "A super contest or something. And we will say a little bit about it each week. That would keep people reading."

"A super contest?" repeated Nancy.

"You know, like . . . like Games Day at school. Only it would be for all the kids in the neighborhood. They could play games and run in races and be in contests. And we will give out blue ribbons."

"And afterward we can write about Games Day and the winners in *The 3M Gazette*!" exclaimed Hannie.

"Oh, that is brilliant," said Nancy.

The Three Musketeers worked extra hard on the next issue of *The 3M Gazette*. We spent two weeks on it. We collected new stories from the kids in the neighborhood. We wrote them up honestly. We made pictures to go with them. We drew up a word search puzzle. We asked everyone for their thoughts about going back to school, and we wrote about them in a story called "Kidspeak." We announced a joke-telling contest. And then, in a little box at the end of the last page, we wrote: *Stay tuned for news about Games Day!* (That is all we said about it.) When we *finally* finished *The 3M Gazette*, our paperboys delivered it.

Nancy and Hannie and I were gigundoly tired.

Games Day

The fourth issue of *The 3M Gazette* was a hit. Everyone liked it — kids, grown-ups, even Mr. and Mrs. Billing and Mr. Papadakis. Even Charlie. My friends and I were not in trouble, and no one thought our paper was too boring or too funny. Finally.

The fifth and sixth issues were hits, too. The kids in the neighborhood especially liked the things they could be a part of. They liked being asked questions for Kidspeak. They liked writing letters to the paper. Best of all, they liked the contests.

Also, they were looking forward to Games Day. In a box at the end of the fifth issue of the paper, we wrote: *Games Day is two weeks from Saturday. Meet in Karen's backyard at 1:00.* In the sixth issue, we printed an article about Games Day. We said that any kid who wanted to have some fun should come to my house at one o'clock. He (or she) should wear sneakers and old clothes. There would be races and games and contests. The winners would get blue ribbons. And Hannie and Nancy and I would write about the afternoon and the kids and the winners in our paper. We were going to make a special issue that was just about Games Day.

I had to ask Kristy to help us with Games Day. "Lots of kids are going to come," I told her. "My friends and I are supposed to be reporters that day. We are supposed to write about everything that happens. We want to interview the winners, too. We need to be able to say things like, 'So, David Michael. You have just won the fifty-yard dash. How do you feel?' We are going to be awfully busy, Kristy."

"Don't worry," Kristy replied. "I will help you on Games Day."

And she did. So did her friends Mary Anne and Bart.

Guess how many kids showed up for Games Day. Fourteen. That was a lot. It was more than I had expected. Luckily, Kristy took charge. (She is good at that.)

"Okay!" she cried. "Everyone who wants to be in the jumping jacks contest, go with Bart. The relay race will be held after that."

Hannie and Nancy and I ran to Bart. Our pencils were poised over our notebooks. We watched the contest closely. When it was over, Bart held up Melody Korman's hand. "And the winner is Melody!" he announced. "Congratulations, champ."

"Where are the blue ribbons?" I hissed to Nancy.

"Right here," she replied. She pulled several out of her notebook. My friends and I had spent hours making blue ribbons out

of cardboard and construction paper.

Nancy ran to Melody and Bart. She handed one of the ribbons to Melody. "Our first winner of the day," she said.

"Hey, Melody!" I called. "You are the first winner at Games Day. How do you feel? What are you thinking?"

I wrote about Melody while Hannie and Nancy covered the fifty-yard dash. Linny Papadakis won the race.

All afternoon the kids played games and ran races. Kristy and her friends had thought of some great contests, especially for the little kids like Sari Papadakis and Emily Michelle. The best one was the "I'm a Little Teapot" championship.

By the end of the day, every kid had won at least one blue ribbon, and most had won several. The big winner was Maria Kilbourne. She left with nine ribbons. "Maybe you should put my picture in your paper," she called as she left the yard.

"Maybe," I replied. My friends and I certainly had a lot of work to do.

Too Much Work

It was Saturday night. Games Day was over. I was in my room at the big house. I was lying on my bed. I was reading another book by the very wonderful Beverly Cleary. It was called *Henry and the Paper Route*. I was trying to enjoy the book, since it was so funny. But the paper route made me think of paperboys, and paperboys made me think of David Michael and Linny, and they made me think of *The 3M Gazette*, and *that* made me think of all the work I had to do.

Boo and bullfrogs.

"Karen?" said Kristy. She was standing in the doorway to my room.

"Yeah?" I replied. "Come on in."

Kristy sat on the end of my bed. "I just want to tell you what a great job you're doing with your paper. And what fun Games Day was. All afternoon I heard the kids saying how much they like *The 3M Gazette*, and how terrific Games Day was, and how they cannot wait to — Karen? What's the matter?"

I had started to cry. I did not know I was going to cry, but suddenly tears were rolling down my cheeks. "Nancy and Hannie and I just finished an issue of the paper," I said, sobbing. "And now we have to write another. And it is probably going to be extra long because it will be about Games Day and all the winners. And I hardly have time for reading anymore."

Kristy looked serious. "Maybe the paper is too much work," she said. "You *have* given yourself a very big job, Karen."

"I know," I replied. I sniffled. "First no

one liked our paper. Now everyone loves it — but I am too tired to write it."

"It might be time to stop," said Kristy. "You have put out six issues of the paper. Maybe that is enough."

"But now the kids look forward to the paper," I wailed. "They like to read about themselves. And they like entering the contests and working on the puzzles. I do not want to let them down."

"Why don't you talk to your father?" suggested Kristy.

So I did. And Daddy and I talked to Elizabeth and Nannie.

"I thought you were having fun with the paper," said Elizabeth.

"I was," I answered. "At first it was like a game. And no one cared whether the paper came out or not. But now the kids expect it. And it is a lot more work. Hannie and Nancy and I do not just write little stories and articles. We make up puzzles, and plan things like Games Day, and pick out the winners in our contests."

"That *is* a lot of work," agreed Nannie.

"I'll say," said Daddy.

"And the problem is," I went on, "that we *promised* we would write about Games Day. The kids are waiting to read about themselves."

We talked and talked. Finally Daddy said, "I have an idea, Karen. Why don't you and Nancy and Hannie put together the issue about Games Day, since you promised you would do that. But that will be the last issue of your paper. I think the kids around here will understand."

"Okay," I said. "Let me call Nancy and Hannie. I have to talk to them."

I called Nancy first. She said, "I was wondering how we were going to write the paper after school started. We would not have had enough time. I was getting worried."

And Hannie said, "Oh, thank goodness. I am really tired of *The 3M Gazette*! I was trying to figure out how to tell you that."

Whew. Why had I been so upset?

Miss Jewel

"Come on, Rocky. Come here. Now sit still. Please behave," I said.

"Karen? What are you doing?" asked Andrew.

It was a late summer afternoon. Andrew and I were playing in the yard at the little house. Rocky and Midgie were with us.

"I want Rocky to wear this bonnet," I said. "I am trying to dress him up. I want to pretend he is going to cat school."

"Boy cats do not like bonnets," Andrew told me.

89

"I guess not." I untied Rocky's bonnet. I let him run away. "Well, I cannot wait for people school to start," I said. "I just love school. I want to see my friends again. I want to see Mr. Mackey. He is the art teacher. And I want to see Mr. Fitzwater. He is the janitor. And I cannot wait to eat in the cafeteria again."

"You are so lucky, Karen," said Andrew sadly.

"I am?"

"Yeah. *You* know all about *your* school. It is not new to you. You have been to it before, and now you get to go back. I cannot go back to my school. I am going somewhere new. I do not know anything about it."

"Andrew," I said, "I think you need to visit your new school."

"Visit it?" he repeated.

"Yes. Then, on the first day of school, it will not seem so new."

That night I told Mommy about my idea.

"I know the schools are closed now," I said. "But do you think Andrew could visit his anyway? And meet his teacher? That would make him feel better."

"Karen, that is a terrific idea. Why didn't I think of that sooner? I will see what I can do."

The next day, Mommy called the school. She talked to Andrew's teacher. And the day after that, we hopped in the car and drove to Littlebrook Preschool. Mommy and Andrew and I.

"Here we are, Andrew," said Mommy.

"Doesn't your school look nice?" I said. "Look at the playground, Andrew. Look at the climbing toys and the sandbox."

Andrew just nodded.

Mommy and Andrew and I walked inside. We found Andrew's classroom. We peeked around the door.

"Good afternoon," said a young woman. She was standing by a table. She was wearing blue jeans and an old paint smock.

"You must be the Brewers. I am Miss Jewel, Andrew's teacher."

My mouth dropped open. Miss Jewel. What a wonderful name.

Miss Jewel put her arm around Andrew. "I am so glad you could visit today. Some of your classmates are also visiting." Miss Jewel pointed to a boy and a girl who were looking at books in the story corner. "They are Sherry Baldwin and Brad Rufus."

"Hey! I know Brad!" exclaimed Andrew. "He went to my old school!" Andrew ran to Brad. "Hi! Hi, Brad!" he cried.

After awhile, Miss Jewel showed Andrew and Brad and Sherry the other things in the room. "Here are the painting easels," she said. "And here is the math cabinet. And here is the imagination center. And here are the art materials." Then Miss Jewel showed them the things on the playground.

Andrew kept calling out, "Hey, look at this!" And, "Cool! Brad, let's play with this." And, "I want to put on a play in the imagination center."

Finally it was time to go home. "Good-bye!" Andrew cried. "Good-bye, Sherry. Good-bye, Miss Jewel. Good-bye, Brad." Mommy and Andrew and I climbed into the car. "I cannot wait for school to start," Andrew announced.

The Children's Page

Andrew did not stop talking about Miss Jewel and his new school. He talked about it for days. He even wanted to play school. "I will be me, and you be Miss Jewel, Karen. Let's put on a play in the imagination center. Okay? Karen? Are you listening?"

I was listening. At least, I was trying to listen. I was very glad Andrew was so excited about his new school now. But I was thinking about something else. *The 3M Gazette.* Nancy and Hannie and I had written our last issue. It was the one about Games Day. And Linny and David Michael had delivered it for us. Most of the stories had been about the kids in the contests and who had won how many blue ribbons. But the very last article on the very last page had been called "The End." My friends and I had written about why *The 3M Gazette* was going to have to stop. We had said we were very gigundoly sorry, but the paper was too much work.

The kids in the neighborhood were sad.

"It was the only interesting newspaper I ever saw," said Melody.

"It was the only newspaper I ever understood," said Linny.

"I had a great new story for you," said Timmy. "My puppy is learning tricks. I wanted to read about that in the paper."

Hannie and Nancy and I felt sad, too. But we did not know what to do. We just could not start writing that paper again.

Then, on the day before school started, the phone rang at the little house.

"I'll get it!" I called. I answered the phone in the kitchen. "Hello?"

"Hello, Karen? This is Mrs. Halsey from the newspaper."

"Oh, hi," I said. "Just a second. I'll get Mommy for you."

"Wait, Karen," said Mrs. Halsey. "I want to talk to you."

"You do?"

"Yes. I have an idea. Your mother showed me several copies of *The 3M Gazette*. And she told me that you and your friends had to stop working on it. That is too bad, because your paper was really very good."

"It was? You liked our paper?" I said.

"Very much," replied Mrs. Halsey. "It made me remember an idea I had a long time ago. I wanted to start a children's page in the *Stoneybrook News*. So yesterday I mentioned the idea to my boss. I told her the children's page would include articles kids would be interested in, and puzzles and activities and so forth. I also suggested that some of the articles be written *by* kids. The kids could be guest writers or reporters. My boss loved the idea. She told me I should start working on it right away."

"That's great," I said.

"So," Mrs. Halsey went on, "I was wondering, Karen, if you would like to write for the children's page. I was hoping you could write a monthly article or column. I will pay you, of course. Would you be interested?"

I hardly knew what to say. "Oh! Oh, yes!" I exclaimed. "I am interested. I am definitely interested!"

"Do you think Hannie and Nancy might want to write for the children's page, too? Just every now and then?"

"I — I think so," I replied. "I will have to ask them, but I think so."

When Mrs. Halsey and I hung up the phone, I sat in the kitchen for a few minutes. I tried to catch my breath. I was so excited. My friends and I would still get to be writers and reporters. We would see our names in print in the *Stoneybrook News*! And the kids in town would soon have their very own page in the paper.

I got right to work. First I called Nancy and Hannie with the news. Then I found my PRESS hat. I sat down to think about my first real newspaper article.

About the Author

ANN M. MARTIN lives in New York City and loves animals, especially cats. She has two cats of her own, Mouse and Rosie.

Other books by Ann M. Martin that you might enjoy are *Stage Fright*; *Me and Katie (the Pest)*; and the books in *The Baby-sitters Club* series.

Ann likes ice cream and *I Love Lucy*. And she has her own little sister, whose name is Jane.

Little Sister

Don't miss #41

KAREN'S SCHOOL

"Andrew!" I called. "Emily! Hurry up. You will be late for school!"

I practically had to carry them into the playroom. Just as they were sitting down, Hannie and Sari arrived.

"Oh, good. You are right on time," I said. "But where are Callie and Keith? And Andrew, where is your homework paper?"

Andrew went looking for his worksheet, while I went looking for Callie and Keith. I found them playing at their house. They had forgotten about Miss Karen's School. And they had not done their homework.

Boo and bullfrogs.

Enter Karen's

B·A·B·Y·S·I·T·T·E·R·S
Little Sister®
Summer Friendship Giveaway!

Karen would never go to camp without her super special stationery kit — and now you can win a kit of your very own! Just fill in the coupon below and return it by October 31, 1993. Each of the **500 winners** will receive a **Baby-sitters Little Sister Stationery Kit** filled with postcards, stickers, a pad, and a sparkle pen!

500 WINNERS!

Rules: Entries must be postmarked by October 31, 1993. Winners will be picked at random and notified by mail. No purchase necessary. Valid only in the U.S. and Canada. Void where prohibited. Taxes on prizes are the responsibility of the winners and their immediate families. Employees of Scholastic Inc.; its agencies, affiliates, subsidiaries; and their immediate families are not eligible. For a complete list of winners, send a self-addressed stamped envelope after October 31 to: Baby-sitters Little Sister Summer Friendship Giveaway, Winners List, at the address provided below.

Fill in the coupon below or write the information on a 3" x 5" piece of paper and mail to:
BABY-SITTERS LITTLE SISTER SUMMER FRIENDSHIP GIVEAWAY, P.O. Box 7500, Jefferson City, MO 65102.
Canadian residents send entries to: Iris Ferguson, Scholastic Inc., 123 Newkirk Road, Richmond Hill, Ontario, Canada L4C 3G5.

- -

Name_____ Date of Birth _____

Street _____

City _____ State/Zip _____

Where did you buy this Baby-sitters Little Sister book?

☐ Bookstore   ☐ Drugstore   ☐ Supermarket   ☐ Library

☐ Book Club   ☐ Book Fair   ☐ Other_____(specify)

BLS793

SPECIAL DELIVERY... FOR YOU!

The Baby-sitters have split up for vacation, but Kristy's in the hospital. How will the girls stay in touch?—A chain letter! Now *you* can open authentically stamped envelopes, unfold and read

Real letters, cards, and even a friendship bracelet from the Baby-sitters Club!

real letters in the baby-sitters' own hand–writing, and learn a special secret about each one of them — all in one spectacular, must-have book!

The Baby-Sitters Club Chain Letter
by Ann M. Martin

Coming in September!

BSCL293

888888888 LITTLE 🍎 APPLE 888888888

BABY-SITTERS

Little Sister™

by Ann M. Martin, author of *The Baby-sitters Club*®

❑ MQ44300-3	#1	Karen's Witch	$2.75
❑ MQ44259-7	#2	Karen's Roller Skates	$2.75
❑ MQ44299-7	#3	Karen's Worst Day	$2.75
❑ MQ44264-3	#4	Karen's Kittycat Club	$2.75
❑ MQ44258-9	#5	Karen's School Picture	$2.75
❑ MQ44298-8	#6	Karen's Little Sister	$2.75
❑ MQ44257-0	#7	Karen's Birthday	$2.75
❑ MQ42670-2	#8	Karen's Haircut	$2.75
❑ MQ43652-X	#9	Karen's Sleepover	$2.75
❑ MQ43651-1	#10	Karen's Grandmothers	$2.75
❑ MQ43650-3	#11	Karen's Prize	$2.75
❑ MQ43649-X	#12	Karen's Ghost	$2.95
❑ MQ43648-1	#13	Karen's Surprise	$2.75
❑ MQ43646-5	#14	Karen's New Year	$2.75
❑ MQ43645-7	#15	Karen's in Love	$2.75
❑ MQ43644-9	#16	Karen's Goldfish	$2.75
❑ MQ43643-0	#17	Karen's Brothers	$2.75
❑ MQ43642-2	#18	Karen's Home-Run	$2.75
❑ MQ43641-4	#19	Karen's Good-Bye	$2.95
❑ MQ44823-4	#20	Karen's Carnival	$2.75
❑ MQ44824-2	#21	Karen's New Teacher	$2.95
❑ MQ44833-1	#22	Karen's Little Witch	$2.95
❑ MQ44832-3	#23	Karen's Doll	$2.95

More Titles... ➡

888888888888888888888888888888

The Baby-sitters Little Sister titles continued...

❑ MQ44859-5 #24 Karen's School Trip $2.75

❑ MQ44831-5 #25 Karen's Pen Pal $2.75

❑ MQ44830-7 #26 Karen's Ducklings $2.75

❑ MQ44829-3 #27 Karen's Big Joke $2.75

❑ MQ44828-5 #28 Karen's Tea Party $2.75

❑ MQ44825-0 #29 Karen's Cartwheel $2.75

❑ MQ45645-8 #30 Karen's Kittens $2.75

❑ MQ45646-6 #31 Karen's Bully $2.95

❑ MQ45647-4 #32 Karen's Pumpkin Patch $2.95

❑ MQ45648-2 #33 Karen's Secret $2.95

❑ MQ45650-4 #34 Karen's Snow Day $2.95

❑ MQ45652-0 #35 Karen's Doll Hospital $2.95

❑ MQ45651-2 #36 Karen's New Friend $2.95

❑ MQ45653-9 #37 Karen's Tuba $2.95

❑ MQ45655-5 #38 Karen's Big Lie $2.95

❑ MQ43647-3   Karen's Wish Super Special #1 $2.95

❑ MQ44834-X   Karen's Plane Trip Super Special #2 $3.25

❑ MQ44827-7   Karen's Mystery Super Special #3 $2.95

❑ MQ45644-X   Karen's Three Musketeers Super Special #4 $2.95

❑ MQ45649-0   Karen's Baby Super Special #5 $3.25

Available wherever you buy books, or use this order form.

Scholastic Inc., P.O. Box 7502, 2931 E. McCarty Street, Jefferson City, MO 65102

Please send me the books I have checked above. I am enclosing $ _____ (please add $2.00 to cover shipping and handling). Send check or money order - no cash or C.O.Ds please.

Name _____

Address _____

City _____ State/Zip _____

Please allow four to six weeks for delivery. Offer good in U.S.A. only. Sorry, mail orders are not available to residents to Canada. Prices subject to change.

BLS1092